This igloo book

belongs to:

....

igloobooks

Published in 2016
by Igloo Books Ltd
Cottage Farm
Sywell
NN6 0BJ
www.igloobooks.com

LEO002 0116
2 4 6 8 10 9 7 5 3 1
ISBN: 978-1-78557-655-3

Printed and manufactured in China

THE BUNGED UP TRUNK

igloobooks

There was to be a concert in the jungle.
The animals were getting prepared.
All except a little elephant,
who was feeling very **scared.**

Elephant was worried. He was filled up with doubt.
"I've never trumpeted before," he said.
"What if nothing comes out?"

"I'll eat some sticky buns," said Elephant.
"I'll have a good **chew.**
They'll make me feel better.
Then I'll know what to do."

Elephant was busy **chewing,** trying to figure things out.
When suddenly, behind him, there was a very **loud** shout.

"Hello, Elephant!"

roared Tiger. He made Elephant jump and suck a whole sticky bun, right up his trunk!

Elephant **waggled** his trunk.
He **waved** it about.

But the bun
wouldn't
budge.

It just **wouldn't** come out.

"Oh, dear," said Tiger.
"You've got a
bun-shaped bump,
that's stopping your trumpet
coming out of your trunk!"

Tiger didn't know whether he
should **laugh** or **cry**.
Then, suddenly, he noticed Cheetah running by.

Elephant tried, he **puffed** and **blew.**
He did everything an elephant could do.

Today he was simply out of luck.
"Let's face it," said Frog.
"Your trumpet is stuck."

"**Help him!**" cried Hippo. "The concert's tonight."
The animals all muttered. They knew Hippo was right.

"**Tickle him!**" said Monkey.
"That should do the trick.
Come on, everyone,
get tickling, **quick!**"

Elephant **chuckled** and **giggled**. He **laughed** until he cried.
But the bun wouldn't move, no matter how **hard** he tried.

"Urgh!" cried the animals.

They were all **dripping** wet
and that stubborn sticky bun hadn't come out yet.
"Hurry up!" cried Hippo. "We've got to work faster.
Otherwise the concert will be a **disaster!"**.

They **jiggled** and **wobbled,** but soon it was clear.
The stuck, sticky bun was not going to appear.

Elephant was **exhausted**. He lay **sprawled** on the floor.

"Let the bun stay," he moaned. "I can't take any more.

I've got no more go. I'm all out of puff.

I'm afraid, my good friends, I've just had enough."

At first Elephant felt **upset,** he felt **silly** and **sad.**

But then, he felt **angry.** He got **red-faced** and **mad.**

"Hold on a minute, Tiger," he said. **"You big, bossy lump.**
It's **YOUR** fault this bun got stuck up my trunk!"
He screwed up his face, like a too-toasted crumpet.
Then, suddenly, Elephant gave a **ginormous...**

The **stuck** bun **shot out** and **whooshed** overhead.
"I knew making him angry would work!" Tiger said.

Elephant got ready for the concert. He couldn't wait to go.
His trumpet was **tremendous,** he was
the **star** of the show.

Elephant was **thrilled** and had so much more fun
because at last he was rid of the **stuck, sticky bun!**